FRIENDS OF ACPL
P9-AOM-382
OCEAN
NORWAY
SWEDEN
LAPLAND
FINLAND
Gulf of Bothnia
Gulf of Finland
Oslo
Uppsala
Mälaren
skerries
Stockholm
Gripsholm Castle
Skansen
Vänern
Dalsland Sound
Vättern
BALTIC
SEA
Skagerrack
skerries
Göteborg
Visby
GOTLAND
Little Karl's Island
ÖLAND
DENMARK
SKÅNE
Copenhagen
0
100
200
Miles

The Skåne boy meets many dangers on his journey.
Earth's animals and Heaven's birds can barely keep him safe.
I, who sent the poor thing on his way,
rejoice over every little friend who gives him refuge,
hides him in his heart.

SELMA LAGERLÖF

The Wonderful Adventure

Text edited by Tage and Kathrine Aurell

Translated by Richard E. Oldenburg

Doubleday & Company, Inc., Garden City, New York

# of Nils

By Selma Lagerlöf

Narrated in pictures by Hans Malmberg

All rights reserved
This book is fully protected by copyright under the terms of the International Copyright Union. Permission to use portions of this book must be obtained in writing from the publisher.
Printed in Sweden
Victor Pettersons Bokindustri AB, Stockholm 1967

CO. SCHOOLS
C690339

The Boy

March 20

Once upon a time there was a boy. He was a rather useless boy. Mostly he liked to sleep and eat and make mischief.

It was Sunday morning, and the boy's parents were going off to church. "Fine," thought the boy, "then I'll go shooting with Father's gun, without anyone to stop me."

But Father seemed to guess his thoughts. "If you don't want to come to church with us, you'll have to read the sermon here at home," he said. Mother quickly brought out the gospel book. "Fourteen and a half pages," she said, "and Father will test you on every one. So start now if you expect to finish it all."

Finally they left. It was the most beautiful spring weather—not yet green, but fresh and budding. But Father and Mother worried about their son, who did not want to learn anything at school, and was lazy and unkind to animals and people. "If only he would change," the mother said sadly.

The boy felt trapped. He began sleepily to skim over the words.

Then he started at a slight noise. Directly in front of him stood a small mirror on the window sill, and in it he saw that the lid of Mother's handsome old chest was open.

Astride the edge sat an elf looking down delightedly on Grandmother's finery.

The boy was not scared—not of one so small. But it might be fun to play a trick on the elf. The boy snatched up a butterfly net and caught him in one sweep. The elf begged frantically to be freed. "I have been good to you for many years," he said. "You will get a silver spoon and a gold coin if you let me go."

The boy agreed, but just as the elf was about to climb out, it occurred to the boy that he might have asked for riches and every conceivable good. He began to shake the butterfly net to make the elf tumble back in again. Right then the boy received such a dreadful box on the ear that he thought his head would crack, and he lay unconscious on the floor.

When he woke up he was alone. The chest lid was down, and the butterfly net was back in its place by the window. But his cheek still burned, so he knew it had been no dream. "I had better read the sermon again," he said and moved toward the table.

But what now?

It was as though the cottage had grown. He had to climb in order to get up to the seat of the chair. He could not see over the table top without clambering onto the armrest. And he had to stand right in the middle of the book to read!

He read a few lines, then happened to glance toward the mirror and cried aloud: "Look, there's another elf!" Because plainly he saw a little chap in pants and pointed cap. "He is dressed like me," the boy said and clapped his hands. But he noticed that the little fellow in the mirror did the same. He pinched his arm and pulled his hair. The boy in the mirror did so too.

Now he was frightened because he understood that the elf had bewitched him and that the little chap in the mirror was himself. "If I wait a little maybe I'll become human again," he thought and closed his eyes. But no. He remained just as small. "I must make friends with the elf," he thought. He began to search but no elf was to be found. He broke into tears and prayed and promised never to lie again, never to be mean, never to fall asleep during the sermon.

Nothing happened . . .

Out in the courtyard, a flock of sparrows caught sight of the boy and suddenly chattered: "Look, look! Look at Nils the Gooseboy! Look at Thumbkin! Nils Holgersson Thumbkin!" Immediately there was a dreadful cackling. "Cock-a-doodle-do," crowed the cock. "Serves him right. He pulled my comb!" "Ka ka ka," shrieked the hens. "Serves him right, serves him right!"

"I've been changed into an elf. I understand what they are saying . . ."

Now a bellowing and mooing was heard from the window, through which the cows were looking. "Mooo! It's a good thing there's some justice in the world!" The boy asked about the elf. "Just come out," May-Rose said. "I will let you dance on my horns."—"I'll pay you for the wasp you let loose in my ear!" bellowed Golden Lily.

"Come here and I will reward you for all the times you snatched the milking stool out from under your mother and tripped her when she was carrying the milk pail, and for all the tears she has shed over you."

The boy tried to say that he was sorry and that he would always be good from now on if they told him where the elf was. But they only shook their heads and waved their horns at him.

He understood that no one on the farm wanted to help him. Even finding the elf would probably do him no good.

What would happen if he never became human again? When Father and Mother came home from church, what would they

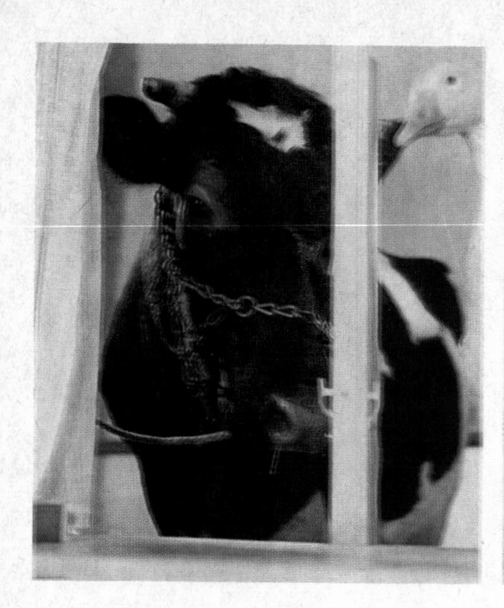

think? The whole countryside would wonder . . . Imagine, no longer to be a human being, but a freak. He looked around his home. Small and poor, perhaps, in the eyes of others, but far too good for him now. He would probably have to live in a little burrow somewhere under the stable floor. Never again would he be happy about anything . . .

It was marvelously fine weather. He had never seen the sky so blue. Birds of passage were on the wing. There were many different kinds, but he recognized only the wild geese, who flew in two long lines, making an angle like a plow. Through the door he could hear their cry. "Now off to the mountains, now off to the mountains!"

The boy remembered his mother's telling him that the little people used to live in the cowshed. He would go there and find the elf. It was fortunate that the cottage door was open, since he could not have reached up to work the lock. Now he slipped through without difficulty.

In the entryway he looked for his wooden shoes because he had of course been walking around indoors in his stocking feet. He wondered how he would manage the big clumsy wooden shoes, but right away he saw a pair of small shoes by the threshold. The elf had been that thorough! The boy became still more uneasy. It seemed that this punishment would last for a long time . . .

Now he heard the wild geese close by. Perhaps they had seen the tame geese on the farm, because they cried, "Come along! Come along! To the mountains, to the mountains!"

But the tame geese answered sensibly enough: "We are content as we are."

An unusually delightful day it was, as we said before; it must have been a real joy to fly. So with each new wild flock that passed, the tame geese became more and more restless. They fluttered and fluttered their wings. "Don't be foolish," said the old mother goose. "Those wild ones will suffer both hunger and cold."

Within one young gander, however, the cries of the wild geese awakened an irresistible longing. When a new flock came and cried, "Come along! Come along!" he answered, "Wait, wait! I am coming."

He spread his wings and rose in the air, but fell back again. He was so unaccustomed to flying . . .

The wild geese turned about and flew more slowly. They wanted to see if he planned to try again.

All this the boy saw and heard while he stood in the door of the entryway.

As he hopped into the wooden shoes, he thought what a pity it would be if the gander flew away. It would sadden Father and Mother when they returned.

Again he forgot that he was small and powerless. He leaped right down among the geese and threw his arms around the gander's neck. "You'd better not fly away, you," he cried.

But just then the gander found the way

to raise himself off the ground. He could not pause to shake off the boy, who was carried along into the air.

The boy gasped. Before he realized, they were so high up that he would have been killed if he had fallen to the ground. The only thing he could do was to scramble up on the back of the goose. Then it was no easy thing to keep his seat on the slippery back between the flapping wings. He had to dig deep into feathers and down with both hands to keep from falling to the ground.

The boy was giddy for a long while. The air whizzed and whirred against him and roared in the feathers like a full gale. Thirteen geese were flying around him, flapping their wings and cackling. Finally he realized that he should find out where the geese were taking him. But he didn't dare to look down, since he was sure he would faint if he tried.

Actually the geese were flying quite low, because their new traveling companion could not breathe in the very thinnest air. For his sake they also flew a bit more slowly

than usual. At last the boy forced himself to glance down toward the earth. Then it seemed to him that beneath him lay spread out a great cloth, divided into an incredible number of large and small squares. Nothing was round or crooked. "What kind of checkered cloth is that?" he said to himself, not, of course, expecting anyone to reply. But he got an answer. "Fields and meadows! Fields and meadows!" the wild geese cried.

What he saw was the flat land of Skåne, in other words. The bright green squares were the fields of rye which had been sown the previous autumn and had stayed green beneath the snow. The yellowish gray were stubble fields, the brown were clover meadows and the black were beet fields or plowed soil. Some squares with gray in the middle were farmsteads, and squares turning green were orchards.

The boy could not help laughing when he saw how checkered everything was. Almost reprovingly, the wild geese cried, "Fertile and good land! Fertile and good land!"

Serious once again, the boy thought, "How can you laugh, you, who have let yourself in for the worst that can happen to a human being!"

Soon he had to laugh again, however.

To ride fast and recklessly was something the boy had always liked, but this kind of speed was new to him. And he had never dreamed that one could feel such freedom and well-being as he felt up here in the air, nor that such a good smell of soil and resin rose from the earth. Nor had he ever imagined what it would be like to travel so high. It was like flying away from every care.

The big tame gander felt very proud and happy as he journeyed over the plains of Skåne in the company of the wild geese. But later in the day he began to tire, and lagged several goose-lengths behind the others.

Then those who flew last called to the lead goose who guided the flight, "Akka, Akka from Kebnekaise! The white one is lagging behind!" —"Tell him it's easier to fly fast than slowly!" the lead goose replied and raced on as before.

And the gander tried hard, but became more and more exhausted.

"Akka, Akka from Kebnekaise, the white one is sinking!" —"Anyone who can't keep up can turn home!" the leader cried.

"Oh, so that's how it is," the gander thought. It was only for fun that they had enticed him to come along. They had never intended to take him with them to Lapland. And most provoking of all, he had met up with Akka from Kebnekaise. Even though he was a tame goose, he had heard of her—that she was more than a hundred years old and was much admired, and that she and her wild flock particularly despised tame geese. He longed to show her that he was their equal. Then the little one he carried on his back said suddenly, "Dear Morten Gander, surely you realize that it's impossible for you, who have never flown before, to go along all the way up to Lapland. Turn around before you destroy yourself!"

At this the gander felt so provoked that he was determined to keep on. "If you say one more word, I will toss you off!" he hissed.

Now the sun was sinking fast, and the geese veered straight down. Before the boy and the gander could say a word, they were standing on the shore of a large lake covered by an ice crust full of holes and cracks.

Akka from Kebnekaise

March 21 – 27

The boy was so miserable that he could have cried. He was hungry and had eaten nothing all day long. Where could he find food? Who would make his bed, warm him, protect him? From the forest came a pattering and rustling. Now the cheerful courage he had felt in the air was gone.

In his anxiety he looked around for his traveling companion. He had no one else to cling to.

But the gander lay as though ready to

die, motionless, with his neck limp and his eyes closed. And the boy, who had previously been so unkind to all animals, became terribly afraid of losing the gander. He started to shove him down into the water. The gander was heavy, but the boy found to his joy that he was almost as strong as before he had been bewitched. The gander was soon in the water. Revived, he swam away toward the reeds. When he returned he had a small fish in his bill. "Here is something for you because you helped me."

It was the first kind word the boy had heard all day, and was almost as welcome as the raw fish. His sheath knife was no bigger than a match now, but it served to scale the fish. The boy ate and felt satisfied.

"It would be an honor for me if I could go along to Lapland," the gander said later, "but I cannot manage alone on such a journey. Will you come and help me?"

The boy had thought that they would surely return home now. But it would certainly be nice not to have to show himself to his parents for a while yet. And he was just about to answer yes when all the wild geese came roaring up from the lake in a long line, with the lead goose at the head.

The lead goose said, "Let us now hear what kind of high and mighty beings you are to wish to join the company of wild geese. Your flying is certainly nothing special. But can you swim and run?"

The gander thought that Akka had already decided to send them home, so he answered, "I cannot run and I have never swum farther than across a marlpit."

"You answer with courage, so you might become a good traveling companion. Stay with us a few days so that we may see what you are worth. But who is it you have with you? What is his name?"

The boy stepped quickly forward. "I am Nils Holgersson and until today I was a human being. But this morning . . ."

All the wild geese immediately moved back three steps and hissed with rage. "Clear out of here! We don't tolerate human beings!"

"You cannot very well be afraid of one who is so small," the gander said soothingly.

It was evident that the lead goose had difficulty overcoming her fear. "I have been taught to distrust all human beings. But if you vouch for this one, he may stay with us tonight. We will sleep on the free-floating ice out there."

Morten did not wish to reveal that the boy was human. "He is called Thumbkin, I think."

The lead goose was very old, but her eyes glowed more clearly and, in a way, more youthfully than those of the others. She now said haughtily, "I am Akka from Kebnekaise. And there stand Yksi from Vassijaure and Kaksi from Nuolja. And here are Kolme, Neljä, Viisi, and Kuusi. The other six goslings are also high-mountain geese of the finest blood. We do not share sleeping quarters with one who dares not tell us from what breed he comes."

"You are wise to choose such a safe place to sleep," Morten said. "But tomorrow I shall be leaving you, because I have promised not to abandon Thumbkin."

"Do as you please," Akka said, and flew with the wild geese out to the ice and went to sleep.

The boy was both distressed and fearful, but Morten only said, "Gather together as much dry grass and chaff as you can."

When the boy brought it, the gander picked him up with his bill and flew out onto the ice. There he settled himself on the dry grass and tucked the boy under his wing. In a moment the boy was asleep. He was so tired—but nice and warm.

He woke suddenly to find himself standing on the ice. Around him the geese were flapping and crying out. He understood nothing until he saw a small short-legged dog scamper away with a goose in his mouth. Instantly the boy rushed after him. And though it was entirely dark he could plainly see all the cracks and holes because he had acquired the good night-vision of an elf. The ice had again drifted toward the shore, from which the dog had come. Rushing after him, the boy plunged into the forest. But it was no dog he was chasing. It was Smirre Fox, a true master thief. At last Nils got hold of the tail of the fox. Smirre pulled him along behind. But when the fox saw how harmless his pursuer was, he stopped and began to tease him. Still the boy jerked as hard as he could, and suddenly the goose was able to flap away and disappear. Smirre was terribly angry and swung around so that the leaves flew, but the boy kept his hold on the tail and hung on and laughed. Then he let go quickly and climbed a tree. Smirre sat down to watch the tree and the boy.

The night became dismal and cold. Nils didn't dare sleep because then he might fall. At last the sun rose, however, and from the lake came the cries of the wild geese. They probably thought that the fox had eaten him up. He was close to tears. Then a wild goose came flying alone, in under the tight roof of trees. Smirre started chasing her. Time and again he leaped and missed her. And then the goose disappeared. When the fox came back the little one too was gone.

Next morning the wild geese passed on to broad fields where they could feed. "You run around too daringly," Akka said to Nils. "Remember that you have many enemies. The fox and the marten in the forest, the otter on the shore, the weasel by the stone fences, the viper in the meadow."

The boy was not afraid of dying, but he had no desire at all to be eaten. An entire week had gone by since he was bewitched, and he was still just as small. He wondered what he would do when the wild geese moved northward soon. Then Akka and the others approached him with unusual solemnity. He understood immediately that they had reached a decision.

"You probably wonder," Akka said, "why I have not thanked you for saving me from Smirre Fox. But action is better than words. I have sent a message to the elf who bewitched you and told him how well you have behaved among us. Now he sends word that as soon as you return home you will become a human being again."

At first the boy was glad. But then, without a word, he turned away and started to cry.

"Did you expect more from me?" Akka asked.

The boy was thinking of adventure and freedom and fun and journeys beneath the heavens.

"I do not wish to become human again!" he cried. "I want to follow you to Lapland."

"You should know," Akka replied, "that the elf is quick-tempered. If you refuse, it will be difficult for me to persuade him again later."

It was a strange thing about Nils Hol-

gersson that he had never really liked anyone. Therefore there was no one he missed or longed for. "I want to go with you to Lapland. That is why I have been good for a whole week," he sobbed.

"I am not refusing you," Akka said, "but there may come a day when you will bitterly regret it."

"No," said the boy. "I have never been so well off as I am here with you. There is nothing to regret."

"Then it shall be as you wish," Akka said.

The boy felt so happy that he had to weep for joy, as a moment before he had wept for grief.

The Great Crane Dance

March 28 – 30

Early one morning the geese, sleeping out on the ice of a lake, were awakened by loud cries from the air. "Trirop, trirop! Trianut the crane sends greetings to Akka. Tomorrow the great crane dance takes place on Kullaberg. Welcome!"

The wild geese were very glad. "You are lucky to attend the crane dance," they said to Morten. —"Is it so remarkable?" asked the gander. —"It is something you have never dreamed of," the wild geese replied.

Kullaberg Mountain is low and long, and thrusts itself far out into the sea. From ancient times the animals have gathered here every year. Their playground is well concealed behind hills and knolls. Each species of animal keeps to its hillock, though of course there is a general truce during the meeting. On that day a baby hare could stray across the hill of the foxes without losing even one of his long ears.

The boy let his gaze wander from knoll to knoll. Above one he saw the antlers of the stags. Above another, the neck crests of the gray herons. One hillock was red with foxes, one black-and-white with sea birds, one brown with hares.

The play began. One hundred wood grouse in shining black-brown attire and with bright red eyebrows cast themselves up into a large oak. They turned up their tails so that the white wing coverts showed. A clucking began deep down in their throats, but soon they closed their eyes and whispered, "Sis, sis, sis. Hear how beautiful. Sis, sis." In a rapture, they lost themselves entirely. And it infected the whole animal host. The blood beat in their veins. "Now the frost of winter is past," they thought. "The fires of spring burn over the earth."

Just as the black cocks, with their beautifully curved tail feathers, rushed out to compete with the wood grouse, something unheard of happened. While the animals were thinking only of the play of the grouse, a fox came sneaking very slowly up to the hillock of the wild geese. He had come a long way up the hill before anyone noticed him. Suddenly, however, a goose caught sight of him and started to cry, "Take care, Wild Geese, take care!" The fox caught hold of her by the throat, perhaps mainly to silence her. But the wild geese had already heard her, and they all rose in flight. When they were in the air, they saw Smirre Fox standing on their hill with a dead goose in his mouth.

Because he had thus broken the truce of the festival day, Smirre was severely punished. He would regret for the rest of his life that he had tried in this way to take revenge on Akka and her flock. He was at once surrounded by a mass of foxes and sentenced according to the old custom which decrees that anyone disturbing the peace on the great festival day must go into exile. No fox wanted to lighten the sentence, since they all knew that the moment they made such a proposal, they would be driven from the

playground forever. Thus Smirre was forbidden to reside in Skåne, and was forced to try his luck in foreign parts. And so that all foxes in Skåne might know that Smirre was outlawed in the province, the eldest of the foxes bit off the tip of his right ear. As soon as this was done, the young foxes started to howl bloodthirstily and threw themselves on Smirre. There was nothing for him to do but flee, and with the young foxes close upon his heels he hurried away.

All this happened while the black cocks and the wood grouse were at their play. These birds had become so absorbed in their song that they neither heard nor saw.

The competition of the forest birds was barely over when the stags appeared to show their war game. There were several pairs fighting at the same time. They hurled themselves at each other, knocked their antlers together thunderingly so that the points got entangled, and tried to force each other backward. From their throats issued frightful roars, and froth poured down to their shoulders.

On the hills all around there was breathless silence as the battle-wise stags clashed with each other. And in all the animals new feelings were awakened. Each one felt courageous and strong, full of a sense of renewed power, born again with the spring, and ready for all kinds of adventure. They felt no unfriendliness toward each other, but everywhere wings were raised, neck feathers reared, claws sharpened. If the stags had continued one moment longer, there would have been wild strife on the hills, for all had been seized by a desire to show that they too were brimming with life, that the winter was over, that strength surged in their bodies.

But the stags stopped fighting at exactly the right moment, and immediately a whisper went from knoll to knoll. "Now the cranes are coming . . ."

Then came the gray, twilight-clad birds with plumes in their wings and red feather ornaments on their necks. High-legged, with slender necks and small heads, they glided downhill in a mysterious trance. And while gliding, they turned about—half flying, half dancing. With wings gracefully raised, they moved with unbelievable speed. It was as though gray shadows played a game learned from the mists that hover over the lonely bogs. There was witchcraft in it, and all those who hadn't been to Kullaberg before understood why the whole meeting took its name from the dance of the cranes. There was wildness in it, yet the feeling it awakened was one of sweet longing. No one thought of combat now. Instead, both the birds and those who had no wings wanted to lift themselves above the clouds, to seek what lay beyond, to leave the weighty bodies which dragged them down to earth and soar away toward the heavens.

This longing for the unattainable, for what lies hidden beyond life, the animals felt only once a year on the day they beheld the great crane dance.

In Rainy Weather

March 30 – April 1

On the very day the wild geese were to set off from the lake, the rain came. The wild geese were glad, because the rain makes holes in the ice roofs on the lakes, but the boy shivered and felt cold.

He bore up courageously, though, and when the wild geese swooped down on a marsh, he ran cheerfully to look for cranberries and frozen lingonberries. But toward evening the wilderness became frightening. If he were not going to die from fright he felt he must have fire and warmth. He had caught a glimpse of a village when the geese landed, and he stole toward it. He heard people talking and laughing within the warm rooms.

Then the boy felt a strange alarm and wanted to cry. He was troubled because he had shut himself out from people. He was suddenly terribly afraid of never becoming a real boy again.

He sat on a staircase in the pouring rain and pondered.

Then an owl flew down onto a nearby tree. A tawny owl under the roof ridge cried: "*Kvitt,* Marsh Owl! How was it abroad?"

"Fine, thank you! And here at home?"

"Well, in Skåne a boy has been transformed into an elf and now he travels on a tame goose to Lapland." —"Remarkable, Tawny Owl. And is he never to be human again?" —"That is a secret, but I'll tell you. The elf has said that if the boy watches over the gander so that he stays safe and sound . . . Hush, let's fly up to the church tower. Perhaps someone is listening here on the village street."

The owls flew away, but the boy tossed his cap high in the air. "Hurrah! I *can* become a human being again! And of course I will watch over the gander!" Happily, he hastened back to the marsh and his traveling companions.

* * *

Neither the wild geese nor Smirre had thought that they would ever meet again after they left Skåne. Smirre had gone and was very dissatisfied with the hunting there. Akka had sent Yksi and Kaksi to scout and they reported ice on all the waters and snow on all the ground. So Akka decided to fly toward the coast where spring comes early.

Then it happened that Smirre, who was hunting in a desolate forest, caught sight of a flying flock of geese, one of which was white . . . He immediately set off in pursuit of them, because he wanted a good meal for one thing, and for another, revenge. But Akka had located a sleeping-place to which no Smirre could come—a narrow strip of

river embankment. In front was a rushing river and behind was the steep mountain wall. Nevertheless, the boy dared not sleep. Under the gander's wing he would not be able to hear any danger that might threaten Morten.

Suddenly he saw in the moonlight the gleam of an eye from a low branch. It was a marten. The boy sent a stone flying, and the marten was so surprised that he fell into the water. All the geese awoke and flew away.

Not until much later did Akka find a new sleeping-place. In the foamy whirlpools below a waterfall, there was a flat

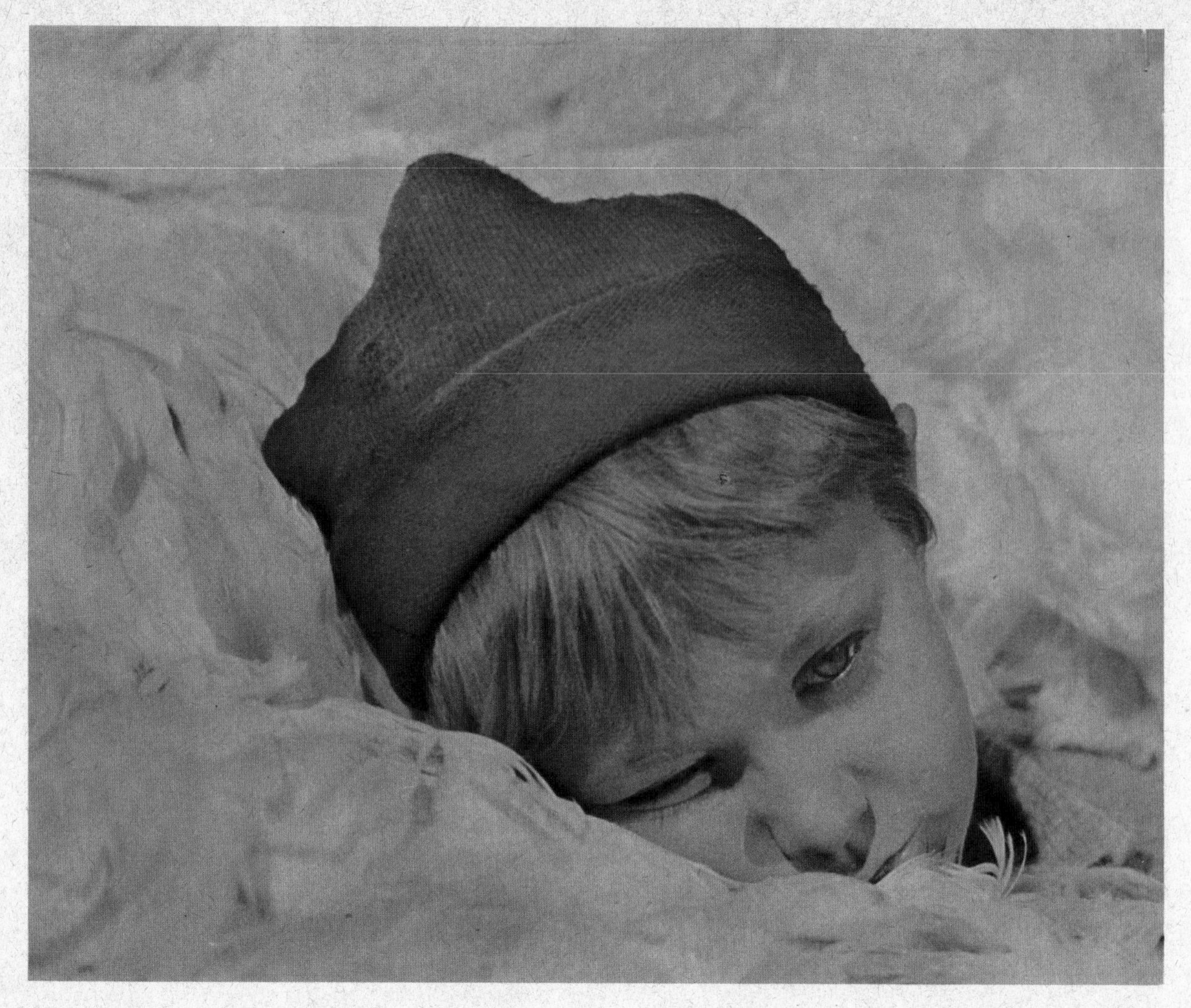

rock, to which no fox or marten could venture. The geese soon went to sleep, but the boy kept watch over the gander.

Through the rush of the water, it suddenly seemed to him that he heard a strange noise. He turned and saw the head and the paw of an otter, which was about to climb up on the skerry. Quickly he drew his sheath knife and stabbed at the paw. The otter lost his foothold and disappeared with a splash into the rapids. They had to find new quarters for the night.

The half-moon still shone when Akka let them land on the deserted balcony of a resort hotel, empty during the winter.

But soon there came a weird howl from the resort park below. On the front lawn in the white moonlight stood a fox. Smirre had followed the geese the whole night, but here he could not reach them and he howled his anger. Akka woke. "Is that you, Smirre?" —"Yes, how do you like the night I have arranged for you?" —"Oh, so it was you who sent the marten and the otter to attack us." —"Yes, it was. And now I will start a foxy game with you wild geese. As long as one of you is alive, I will pursue you across the entire country. But if you prefer to throw down that Thumbkin to me, I promise not to chase you further." —"I will not give you Thumbkin," Akka answered. "We will defend him with out lives." —"If you love him so much," Smirre said, furious, "then he will be the first one I take my revenge on." And Smirre disappeared with an angry yowl.

The boy was still lying awake, and now it was Akka's words to the fox which kept him from sleeping. Never had he believed that he would hear anything so grand as that someone would risk his life for his sake.

And from that moment it could no longer be said of Nils Holgersson that he didn't like anyone else.

Karlskrona

April 2

The naval base of Karlskrona lay lonely in the moonlight as the wild geese came looking for a sleeping-place safe from Smirre the fox. Against the glass-green sky, the town seemed an enchanted island. They saw the church with two square towers, on one of which the geese swooped down. But after only five minutes' sleep, the boy slid out from under the gander's wing and climbed down to the ground.

Luckily no one was in the square. There was only a bronze statue, with a severe face, a hooked nose, an ugly mouth, and a thick cane in its hand. All at once the boy felt

weak and forlorn and tried to cheer himself up by being funny. "What's that longlip doing here?" he said and walked farther along the square. Then he heard heavy steps following him over the cobblestones, so that the ground trembled and the houses shook. The boy was frightened. "Perhaps it is the bronze man," he thought and turned into a side street. The bronze man followed. In front of a small wooden church a man stood and beckoned. The boy was glad and hurried over to him. Then he saw that the man was only a wooden poor box . . . and now the bronze statue had come quite near. At that very moment the wooden man bent down to the boy and stretched out his broad hand. In one leap the boy was up in it, and the wooden man tucked him under his hat. Barely was the arm back in its place again before the bronze man halted and asked in a ringing voice, "Who are you?" The arm of the wooden man moved up in salute, so that the old wood creaked. "Rosenbom, may it please Your Majesty. Boatswain on the lineship *Boldness*. Afterwards a church verger and now a poor box carved in wood." The boy felt shaken when he heard the wooden man say, "Your Majesty." Then the statue must be no less a person than Charles the

Eleventh, the King who had founded the city.

"Have you seen anything of a little brat running around here tonight? If I can only get my hands on the rascal, I shall teach him some manners!" the King said angrily and thumped with his cane. —"Oh yes," the wooden man replied, "he ran to the shipyard and hid there." —"Then come with me, Rosenbom. Four eyes see more than two." —"I may look strong because of the fresh paint, but I am decayed and old." But the bronze man gave the wooden one a resounding thump on the shoulder. "You come along, Rosenbom. You will see that you can take it."

With that, the two formidable figures

set off through the streets of Karlskrona, and the boy peeped through a chink in the wooden hat. The King kicked open the gate to the shipyard. The bronze man and the wooden man enjoyed the sights like two old salts, and the boy sat secure under the wooden hat. Finally they came to the yard where the figureheads from old ships-of-the-line stood mounted: great, terrifying faces full of a proud boldness. There the bronze man said with authority, "Take off your hat, Rosenbom. All these have been in battle for their country." Rosenbom, like the bronze man, had forgotten why they had begun their wandering. Without thinking, he raised the wooden hat from his head and cried, "I lift my hat to the man who chose the harbor and re-created the navy, to the King!" —"Thank you, Rosenbom. You are a splendid fellow. But what is this, now?" For there stood Nils Holgersson in the middle of Rosenbom's bald pate. He raised his red cap and shouted in his turn: "Hurrah for you, Long-lip!" The bronze man struck his cane on the ground, but the boy never knew what he had intended to do, because now the sun rose. At once both bronze King and wooden man disappeared as if they had been mist. While the boy still was staring after them, the wild geese flew over the city. Quickly the white gander caught sight of Nils Holgersson and darted down to fetch him.

Voyage to Öland

April 3 – 6

The wild geese went out to an island to feed. There they encountered some gray geese who were much astonished to see their kinsfolk so far out among the seaward skerries. Akka told them of Smirre Fox. An old, wise gray goose said, "It is a great misfortune for you that the fox was outlawed in his own country. Now he will pursue you all the way to Lapland. Take the outer route to the island of Öland and stay there a few days so that Smirre will be confused and lose the scent." This, Akka thought, was good advice.

It was as calm and warm as summer, just right for a voyage. The sea stretched out as smooth as glass, so that it seemed to the boy that the water had disappeared. He had heaven and clouds both above and below him and was quite giddy. He clung to the goose's back more anxiously than when he had sat there for the first time. And things got worse when they reached the great flight-track of the migratory birds. Thousands of birds flew along a fixed route—wild ducks, graylags, scoters, guillemots, loons, long-tailed ducks, mergansers, grebes, black-billed magpies, and black grouse. The boy saw the whole bird procession mirrored in the water and became so dizzy that he imagined the droves of birds were flying upside down. "Perhaps we are traveling all the way up to heaven," he thought, and felt all at once enormously glad because he was leaving the earth.

Then a couple of shots cracked out, small white columns of smoke rose from the ground, and he heard the worried birds cry, "Hunters! Hunters in the boats! Fly high!" Oh no, they were not in heaven at all! In a long row lay small boats filled with hunters. One shot sounded after another. Small dark bodies sank down toward the sea and cries of anguish rose from the living as they steered toward the heights as quickly as they could. The wild geese got off safely, but the boy was dismayed to think that anyone would want to shoot at such as Akka and Yksi and Kaksi. The men did not know what they were doing . . .

Before they reached Öland, a light wind came up, sending great masses of white vapor toward them. It billowed more and more densely, a damp fog. Soon they could not see one goose-length ahead. The other birds, who knew the route well, started to play in the fog, trying to lure each other astray. The wild geese were tricked time and again, so that Akka became quite flustered. "Why are you here?" a swan shouted. "Come, and I will show you the right way." And when he had lured them far away from the others, he disappeared in the fog. "Don't you see that you are flying upside down?" a duck cried, and the boy grasped the neck of the gander. It was something he had long been afraid of.

Then a hollow, rolling shot was heard from afar and Akka stretched her neck forward, snapped hard with her wings and drove on at full speed. The geese knew that on the southernmost cape of Öland stood a cannon which the men used for shooting at the fog. Now Akka knew the direction, and no one in the world would be able to lure her astray.

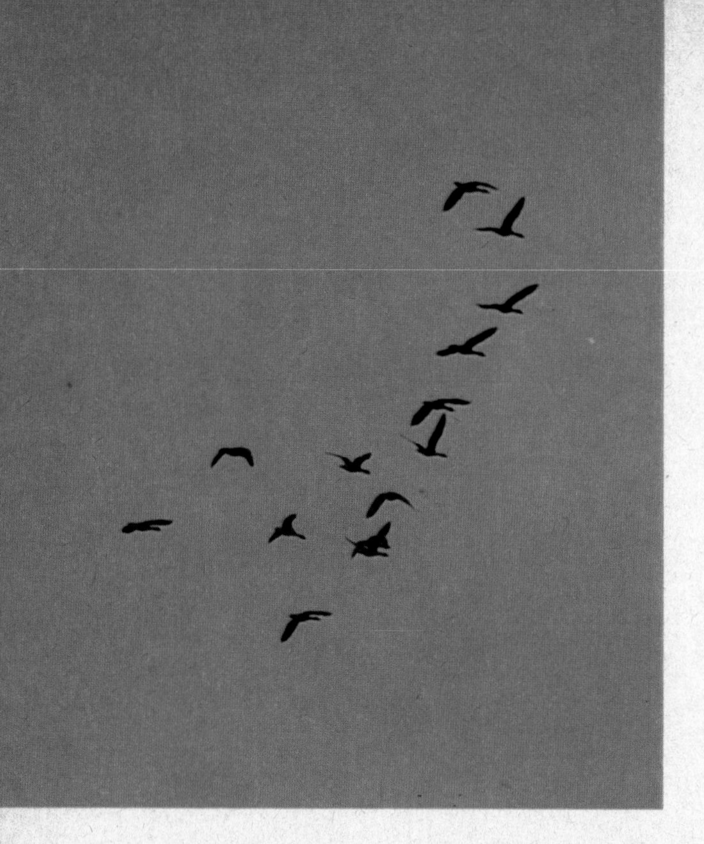

On the southern part of Öland lies an old royal estate. Wild animals are protected there and it is a haven for many thousands of migratory birds.

When the wild geese and Nils had finally found their way to Öland, the fog still lay thick over the island. The boy was amazed at all the birds he could see on only a small stretch of the shore. One and all they wanted only to stay and eat and enjoy themselves in this lush bird paradise.

Next morning it was still just as foggy. The boy walked along the shore's edge and collected mussels. It might be a good thing to take along some food for the journey, he thought. He found some old sedge grass which was tough and strong, and from that he plaited a knapsack. This took him several hours, but he was well satisfied with his work.

At dinnertime the geese came running and cried, "The white one has disappeared in the fog!" The boy felt terribly frightened. "Have you seen any fox or eagle or man or other dangerous creature?" he asked. No, they had seen nothing. The gander had gone astray in the fog, they thought.

The boy set out at once to search. "Morten! Morten! Where are you?" he cried. He searched until it began to get dark, but all in vain. What would become of him if he didn't find Morten? There was no one it would be more painful for him to lose.

As he wandered sadly back across the meadow, what whitish thing emerged from the fog if not the gander! "The whole day I have wandered around and around," Morten said. —"You must promise never to go away from me again!" And the boy threw his arms around Morten's neck. —"No, never. I promise," replied the gander.

But the next morning the geese came running to the boy once more. The gander had disappeared again! And again the boy set out in great distress and shouted and searched along the shore and on the uplands. At night he returned dispirited and tired and could only believe that now Morten had disappeared forever.

Then he heard a rock fall and thought he saw something moving in a heap of stones. He stole closer and saw the white gander laboriously climbing the stone heap with a big bunch of root fibers in his mouth. Morten did not see the boy, who thought there was reason to investigate.

A young gray goose cried for joy when the gander appeared. The boy stole closer so that he could see and hear better. The young graylag had injured one of her wings. She could not fly, and now her flock had left her. She would surely have died of hunger if the gander had not carried food to her. "Good night to you," Morten said. "I will not be gone long, and tomorrow I'll come back. I'm sure you'll soon be well."

"There can be no talk of your staying here," the boy thought of saying. But when he caught sight of the graylag, he understood Morten. She had a beautiful little head, and her eyes were mild. "Don't be afraid of me," the boy said when she tried to run away. He saw that her left wing was out of joint. "I am Morten's traveling companion." When the young goose heard this, she lowered her head gracefully and said

with a voice that was beautiful and soft, "Then I am glad that you came. From the white gander I have learned that no one is as wise and good as you are." The boy became quite bashful.

Yet he felt a great desire to help her. He put his small hands in under her feathers and groped along the wing bone. Nothing was broken. He took a grip on the bone and fitted it into the empty socket. Considering that it was his first attempt, he certainly did it very well. But the poor young goose uttered a piercing shriek and sank down on the stones as though dead.

The boy was terribly frightened. He had wanted to help the goose and now it seemed she was dead. He ran away, feeling as though he had killed a human being.

Next morning the weather was clear, and Akka decided that they should continue the journey. This made the boy happy. He was conscience-stricken and had said nothing to the gander about the graylag. But he wondered if Morten would have the heart to leave her behind . . .

They began the flight. But suddenly the white one turned. The thought of the young goose had overwhelmed him.

With a few wingstrokes, Morten was back at the stone heap. But there was no young goose lying among the stones. "Down-Fine, Down-Fine! Where are you?" the gander cried anxiously. "A fox must have been here and taken her," the boy thought. But at the same moment he heard a beautiful voice answer the gander. "Here I am, here I am!" And up from the water the little graylag came, healthy and sound, and told him that Thumbkin had set her wing in place and that she was quite well and ready to come along on the journey.

The water drops lay like pearl-dew on her silky, shining feathers, and Thumbkin thought once again that she was really like a little princess.

Now in the sunshine they flew the length of the island and the boy was as content as he had been gloomy the day before.

Little Karl's Island

April 8

The wild geese spend the night on the northern cape of Öland on their way to the mainland. But when they neared the first skerries they heard a mighty rumbling and the water below them all at once became completely black. The geese descended swiftly, but before they reached the water, the storm caught up with them from the west and tossed them away toward the open sea. When the geese descended, they found that the sea-green waves rolled high, with seething foam on their crests. This, the wild geese liked. They allowed themselves to be washed up on the wave crests and down into the valleys between the waves and had as much fun as children on a swing. The poor land birds drifting past up in the storm cried enviously, "There is no problem for you who can swim!"

Nevertheless, the wild geese were not out of danger. They became hopelessly sleepy from this rocking, and Akka had to call out constantly, "Do not sleep or you will get lost from the flock!"

But still, many did go to sleep. Akka herself had come close to dozing off when she suddenly saw something round and dark rise above a wave crest. "Seals! Seals! Seals!" she cried shrilly, and all rose into the air with clattering wingstrokes. The seals were so near that they snatched at the feet of the last goose.

All at once the roar grew even stronger than before, it seemed to the boy. Right in front of him he saw, at a few yards' distance, a barren, scraggy rock face. The geese were flying straight toward the cliff!

Then he saw the half-circular opening to a cave, into which the geese steered.

And the next moment, they were safe.

The first thing the travelers thought of was to see whether all had been saved. It seemed that Kaksi had disappeared. But

this was taken lightly. Kaksi was old and wise. She would surely hunt them up.

They were rejoicing over the fine shelter they had found, when Yksi saw some gleaming green dots in the darkness of the cave. "Those are eyes," Akka said in terror, and the geese hurled themselves toward the opening. But Thumbkin, who could see better than the geese, called them back. "This is nothing to be afraid of; it is only some nice sheep."

The geese greeted them and curtseyed. "Please pardon us for barging in this way," Akka then said, "but we are weather-driven and in great need of a safe place to sleep." There was heavy sighing among the sheep and one ewe said, "It is *not* safe here. But before you leave, may we not offer you something?" and she indicated a pool of water and a heap of husks and chaff. This, of course, was a real treat, and the geese pounced on the food. Then they wanted only to sleep. But a big ram said, "This is Little Karl's Island. Only we sheep and some sea birds live here. We manage for ourselves and live in the caves the year round. Here there is ample space for us. But this winter it was so cold that the sea froze, and three foxes came over on the ice. They steal up on us when we're asleep, and they have torn and killed almost all of us. We are the only ones left, and soon we won't have the strength to watch anymore." The ram sighed. Even so, Akka was not very willing to go back out into the storm. She turned to Thumbkin and asked him to keep watch outside the cave.

The boy was only moderately happy over the assignment, even though it was better than being up in the air just then. Soon he saw three foxes stealing up the steep slope. He pulled the big ram by the horns and swung himself up on his back. "Get up, Papa! We are going to frighten foxes!" The foxes had halted in the cave opening, but now they stole closer. "Butt straight ahead!" the boy whispered in the ear of the ram. The big ram butted, and the first fox was thrown whirling out. "Butt to the left!" The boy steered, the ram measured out a dreadful blow, and the second fox rolled down the slope. The third fled. "Now I think that they have had enough for tonight," the boy said. —"That they have," replied the ram. "Now go to sleep in the wool on my back."

The next day, the ram went around with the boy on his back and showed him Little Karl's Island. It resembled a big, round house with straight-up walls and a flat roof. "But if you walk alone here you must look out for the crevices. If you fall down, you are done for." Everywhere on the shore there were remnants of the foxes' meals. They were real criminals, tearing to death many more creatures than they needed to eat. The boy was horrified. "One who is as small and shrewd as you are can put many things right," said the ram. "I shall have to ask Akka and Morten for advice," Nils thought.

Somewhat later the great white goose wandered out carelessly, with Nils on his back.

Neither of them seemed to notice that the three foxes had also come up on the plateau. Morten walked with a limp and had one wing trailing. When the foxes were so close that they were gathering themselves for the final leap, the gander tried to lift himself into the air. The poor thing ran as fast as he could and saved himself at the last moment, while the boy yelled teasingly, "So you have eaten yourself so fat on mutton that you cannot catch up with a goose!" The foxes became mad with rage. The gander raced straight for the deepest cleft in the rock. There he beat once with his wings and made it across. "You can stop, Morten," the boy said when the gander had run a few yards on the other side. Behind them they heard wild cries and heavy falls. But of the foxes they saw nothing more.

The Two Cities

April 9 – 15

That night the wild geese slept out on the plateau, and the boy lay in the short, dry grass. The moon was full and round. The boy remembered that it was Easter Eve. "It is tonight that all the old Easter witches come home." He laughed to himself. He was a little afraid of the elf, but witches he did not believe in at all. In a little while he saw something like a black bird outlined against the moon disk. Soon the stork, Mr. Ermenrich, stood beside him and asked if he wanted to come along on a flying trip in the beautiful moonlight. The boy was delighted that the stork had sought him out, and they flew off out to sea and landed on a desolate shore with even, fine sand. Mr. Ermenrich drew up one leg and said, "I want to sleep a little now. You may look around in the meantime, but do not go too far."

Nils thought that he might climb a hillock of sand and see how the country beyond it looked. Then his wooden shoe struck something hard. It was a thin, tarnished copper coin in the sand. But that was nothing to have; he only kicked it away. Then, as he looked up, he was astounded. Two steps away rose a high, dark wall with a big turreted gate. The whole glittering sea was hidden by the wall! The boy of course understood that there was witchcraft involved, but he very much wanted to know what was behind the gate and quickly entered . . .

He arrived at a vast, stone-paved square with tall houses all around. There was a swarm of people—men in fur-trimmed cloaks over silk clothing, with plumed berets on their heads, and women in long skirts and high hats. The gabled houses were gaily decorated with pictures made of colored glass and black-and-white marble. The cathedral had three huge towers and inside it was filled with gold and color

and burning candles. Outside in the market place stood the merchants selling silk, cloth-of-gold, and lace as sheer as a cobweb.

There a merchant caught sight of him and began eagerly to spread out magnificent goods, tempting him to buy. When the boy shook his head the merchant only became more eager and held up one finger. "Does he mean that all this costs only one coin?" Nils wondered. Suddenly all the merchants were pressing around him and indicating, with tears in their eyes, that one single coin would be enough. Then he remembered the coin in the sand. He ran out to search for it—found it too—and began to hurry back. But the city was gone . . . He saw only the sea before him.

Then he felt the stork prod him with his bill. "I believe you are standing there sleeping, just like me," said Mr. Ermenrich. "What city was it I saw?" Nils asked. "You have been dreaming," the stork answered. "All the same, I will not conceal from you that Bataki the raven claims that once the magnificent city of Vineta stood here. As punishment for the arrogance of its inhabitants, it was sunk to the bottom of the sea. Only for one hour every hundred years is it allowed to rise up again in all its glory. If one merchant had succeeded in selling one thing to you, Thumbkin, the city would have been allowed to remain on the earth and its people to live and die as we and all others." —"Then it was that city I

saw," Nils said. "You brought me here, Mr. Ermenrich, in order that I might save it. And then I couldn't . . ."

He put his hands over his face and cried.

* * *

For two days the boy was completely unlike himself and did not say one cheerful word. He could only grieve over his failure to save the glorious city.

Both Akka and the gander said it had been a dream or an illusion, but he could not believe them and was deeply depressed.

Just then Kaksi came back to the flock, and she knew how to handle this. "There is no need for Thumbkin to mourn an ancient city. Just come with me," she said. So the wild geese said farewell to the sheep and flew to Gotland. Nils sat and looked down on the flat island, and no one can describe how astonished he was. On the shore he saw a city with walls and towers, churches and gabled houses standing quite black against the light sky. It looked just as magnificent as the one he had seen on Easter Eve. But soon he perceived that there was a difference. In this city which had been permitted to remain on land, the high church towers were without roofs, the windows gaped empty, the floors were covered with grass. The glittering splendor was gone. When he stood and washed on the shore, he thought, "No more grief. For who knows whether the sunken city would not have become as tattered as this one. It is better that Vineta remains in all its glory down in the deep."

The wild geese had a good journey across the sea. When they settled down that night,

Akka noted that spring had made much progress. The wild geese were afraid that they had lingered too long in the south, and next morning Akka set their course directly for the bald pate of Taberg mountain. The first to see the wild geese this beautiful spring morning were some miners. One miner stopped drilling for a moment and gaily shouted, "Where are you going?" The geese of course could not understand what he said, but the boy cried with all his might, "Where there are neither pickaxes nor hammers!" The man stared upward with astonishment. He thought that it must be his own longing which made him understand the geese so well...

The geese continued on, over a match factory. At an open window stood a woman worker with a huge matchbox in her hand. "Where are you traveling?" she cried. And the boy called back gaily, "Where there is need for neither matches nor candles!" From a schoolyard came the same cry, "Where are you traveling?" And from Thumbkin, "To a place where there is neither school nor homework!" For he was very happy this lovely spring morning, glad to be so free and lighthearted.

Gripsholm Castle

April 24 – 25

Soon the wild geese came to Lake Mälar. On a point the boy saw a large and splendid red castle raise its massive round towers high above the treetops. The geese descended to feed, and Nils, curious, ran up toward the castle. The great gate by the moat was closed, but a whole school class was sitting and waiting for the guard to open it. The boy saw the teacher put down his jacket. Then he stole into one of the pockets. The jacket was thrown over a shoulder when the guard came, and with that the boy too was inside the castle. The group crossed a courtyard, into great old-world halls where all the walls were covered with tall, dark pictures of serious gentlemen and ladies in peculiar, stiff costumes.

On the second floor, the rooms were lighter, with nothing but grand portraits of kings and queens. On the top floor, they were shown a small theater. Right next to it was a jail with bare stone walls and floors worn by the heavy steps of prisoners there at Gripsholm Castle.

As the class was leaving the castle, the teacher put his hand into the pocket of his

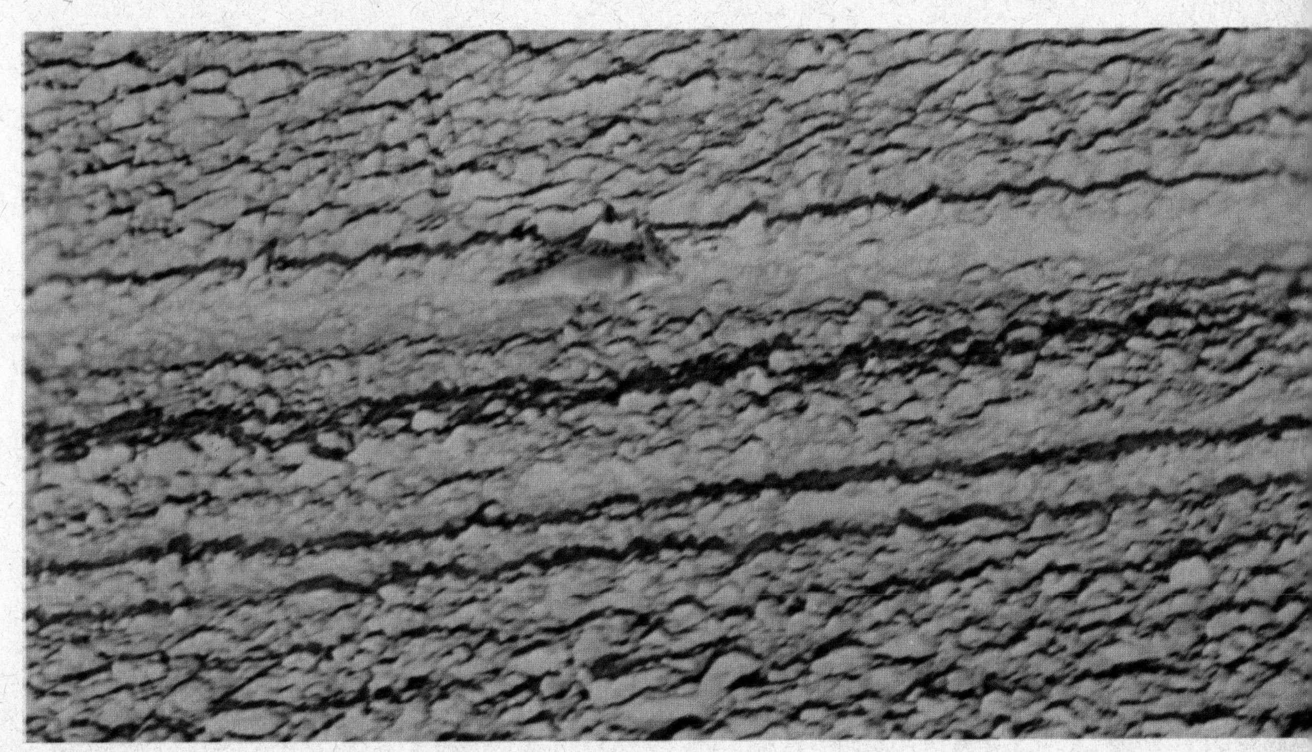

jacket, and accidentally got hold of the boy. But so terrified did he become when he saw the imp that he dropped him. With a bound the boy disappeared among the legs of the schoolchildren and escaped back to the geese again.

The following day they had not been flying long when Nils saw something dark which moved on the ground beneath them. At first he thought it was a dog and would not have given it another thought, except that it kept to the same course as the geese. "It looks like Smirre the fox," the boy thought now. And the next moment the geese changed their course in a wide curve.

"Surely it is Smirre the fox," the boy said to himself. "Therefore Akka is taking another direction."

That night the geese settled themselves for sleep on an island in a lake. The wind was blowing ice-cold now, so the boy crept in under the gander's wing. He was awakened by thundering gunshots and tumbled out terrified. Was he seeing ghostly visions as he had in Vineta? Everywhere, along the shores and on the hills, blazed tall fires. Guns cracked and rockets rose shining toward the sky. "It's the human children at play," Akka said and went to sleep again. The boy heard singing and laughter and music. Like a small mosquito, he was drawn to light and warmth. How gladly

he would have joined them over there and taken part in welcoming the spring. Shivering with cold he crawled back under the wing.

Next morning the sun shone, but the ground was frozen. The geese found nothing to eat and had to fly back toward the southeast. The church bells tolled for services. They could be heard everywhere. The very air seemed transformed into tones. "One thing is certain," the boy reflected. "Wherever I go in this country, I will encounter tolling bells like these." And he felt secure in the thought that he would never be altogether lost, so long as the ringing bells could summon him back.

The Breaking Up of the Ice

May 3 – 4

For several days the weather was terrible, but afterwards the snow melted. Water dripped and rippled everywhere in the fields. The spring brooks began flowing and in many places floods threatened the dwellings of both animals and men.

Before the wind calmed, the wild geese had been driven back to the shore of Lake Mälar. It was warm in the sun. Nils took off his sweater, dried it, and tied it around the neck of the gander, who was moving about feeding, with Down-Fine at his side.

Down-Fine's parents lived on an islet farther out among the seaward skerries. Now she asked the wild geese very sweetly if they would journey to her home so that she might show her family that she was alive. "When she asks for something, not even Akka can say no," said Morten. The visit would only delay the journey a single day.

That night when the wild geese had found their sleeping-place, Nils was too hungry for sleep. "I simply must try to enter some cottage and get myself a little food," he thought.

He jumped out on a stump of board, fished up a small stick, and poled himself toward the shore. He had barely landed when he heard a splashing in the water. He kept still and then saw a female swan lying asleep in her nest a few yards from him. And then! A four-legged creature was stealing up on the swan's nest. At the top of his voice, the boy called, "Hey, Hey!" and beat the water with the stick. The swan arose, though not so quickly that the fox would not have had time to pounce upon her if he had wanted to.

But Smirre instead rushed straight for the boy. Thumbkin dashed off inland. He saw meadows in front of him without a tree to climb, without a hole to hide in. To be sure, he was a good runner, but it was also clear that he could not compete with a fox who had nothing to drag along as he had had the first time.

Then a dog barked. In the nearest farmyard, a huge, handsome watchdog stood in front of his kennel. The boy said in a low voice, "Listen, Watchdog, will you help me catch a fox tonight?" The watchdog did not see well and had become ill-tempered from being kept on a chain. "Are you trying to make fun of me?" he barked. "Just come within reach and I will teach you.

Nobody jokes with me!" —"I am not afraid," said the boy and ran up to the dog, who was so startled that he remained silent. "I am Thumbkin who travels around with the wild geese. Have you heard tell of me, perhaps?" —"Yes, the sparrows have twittered a little, I think," replied the dog. "You seem to have done great things, little though you are." —"Oh yes, I have been doing fairly well," the boy said, "but now I'm finished unless you help me. I have a fox close on my heels. He is lurking around the corner, over there." —"I smell him," said the dog. "That one we will soon get rid of." And the dog barked with all his might. "More is needed than an impressive bark to frighten that fox. He will be back soon. We must figure out how to catch him, you and I." The boy and the watchdog crept into the doghouse and lay there for a long time, whispering.

At last they saw the fox stick his nose out by the corner of the house. Then the watchdog growled, "Go away, or I'll catch you!" —"I think I'll sit here as long as I like in spite of you," replied the fox. "I know how far your chain reaches." —"Blame yourself then!" snarled the dog. And with that, he threw himself in a long leap toward the fox. He reached him without difficulty, for the boy had unbuckled his collar. Thereafter the affair was soon settled. The fox lay on the ground and dared not move. "Yes, keep still," said the dog, "because otherwise I'll bite you to death!" He took the fox by the neck and dragged him to the kennel. There the boy came with the dog chain and wrapped the collar twice around the fox's neck and drew it tight so that he was securely tied. During all this the fox had to lie still, not daring to move.

"Well, Smirre, now I hope they can make a good watchdog of you," said the boy.

Uppsala

May 5

Nils Holgersson was sunning himself on a tuft of marigolds when Bataki the raven landed among the gay flowers. He looked gloomy and somber, but the boy thought he detected a mischievous glint in his eye and decided to be on his guard.

"As a reward for capturing Smirre," the raven said, "I shall tell you a secret. I happen to know what you must do to become a human being again."

Bataki probably thought that Nils would

nibble immediately at such bait, but in reply the boy said that he already knew. If he could bring the white gander to Lapland and back home to Skåne in one piece, then . . .

"But if something goes awry, then perhaps another way out is needed," Bataki said. "Of course I can keep silent . . ." —"Let me hear your secret, then." —"That you shall, when the right moment arrives. First, come with me on a little trip." The boy hesitated, because he was not quite sure where he stood with the raven. "Oh, you don't dare?" These words Nils did not care for, and in the next moment he was sitting on the raven's back.

First they bore off to the university city of Uppsala. That same evening the great spring festival was to be held. From a tower Nils looked down on the students in their white caps marching along by the thousands. The students sang and laughed. There were speeches, and merry dancing—yes, it must be glorious to belong with them!

When everything was over, the boy rubbed his eyes. For a short while he had been in a land of gaiety and now he felt all the more how strange his own life had become. Suddenly he no longer wanted to return to his poor traveling companions.

Then the raven started to croak again. "I shall tell you the secret, Thumbkin. You should wait until you meet someone who says to you that he would gladly be in your shoes and travel about with the wild geese. Then you should say the following . . ." And Bataki whispered a few words in his ear, words that were so strong and dangerous that they could not be spoken aloud, unless one wanted to use them in deep earnest. "Well, that is not likely to help me much," said the boy. "Find some food for me instead. I am so terribly hungry."

The raven did not reply but deposited Nils on a roof outside an attic room. Inside, a lamp was burning, although the student who rented the room was lying asleep. The window was ajar, and on the table were a cup and a half-eaten sandwich. "Thank you, Bataki," the boy said happily and crept inside. Soon he was blissfully feasting

on the sandwich. Neglecting caution, he smacked his lips contentedly.

"Hello, who are you?" a voice said. Terrified, Nils started to flee, but the student looked quite nice. "Nils Holgersson is my name, and I am human although I have been transformed into an elf and am now traveling with the wild geese," he replied boldly. "How very strange," said the student, and started to ask about all that had happened. Finally he said, "Oh, to be in your shoes and get away from all my worries!" Bataki rapped on the window pane with his bill. Nils understood what he meant and said, "You wouldn't want to be anything else." —"Oh, if you only knew all that has happened to me today," the student sighed. "I am finished. I am so unhappy!"

The boy felt giddy and his heart pounded. It almost sounded as though the student had happened to say the right words . . . "Please tell me about yourself now that I have told you my story," he said.

Well, the student had awakened, happy enough. In a few hours he was to have his last examination and after that his life stretched brightly before him. But then a timid and poor fellow student arrived with a heavy manuscript, a book he had written. "Read it, and tell me if it is good enough," he said. "But be careful with it, because I have worked on it for five years and cannot replace it." The student promised. He felt flattered by the older student's confidence. Immediately he began to turn over the leaves and read, page after page. "The fellow is a whiz of a scholar," he said to

himself. "When this book is printed, his fortune will be made. It will be a pleasure telling him so." Then it was time for his examination, and he ran out into the hall for his coat. But in the cross-draft the window flew open, and all the pages on the table were whirled out across the roofs in the spring breeze . . .

In despair, the student rushed forward. Some of the sheets were still lying on the roof. He would no doubt have been able to save part of the lost manuscript had he not had the examination. "It is a matter of my entire future," he thought, and looked with annoyance at a raven sitting on the roof.

He was so upset that all his knowledge seemed to vanish into thin air. He failed the examination. Desperate, he dashed home. Not one sheet was still out on the roof. "I cannot bear to think that I have brought a comrade such misfortune!" the unlucky student concluded. "It would be much better for me if I were in your shoes and could fly away with the wild geese." Bataki rapped again loudly, but the boy sat silent a long time. "Wait a little," he said then in a low voice and walked out through the window. The sun rose, making all the turrets and towers glow and glitter.

"What is the matter with you?" the raven said. "You are missing your chance to become human again." —"I do not care to change places," Nils said. "I would only have trouble because of those wind-blown papers." —"I'm sure I can get them back for you," said Bataki. "I'm sure you can, but I'm not so sure you'll really do it," said Nils.

The raven flew off and returned with one sheet, then another and still another. "Now they are all here," he panted at last, and saw at the same moment that the student was already putting the pages in order. "You are the biggest blockhead I have come across," the raven screamed at Nils. "If you have given him the book, he will never change places with you!" The boy in his turn watched the happy student. "Thank you, Bataki," he said. "I understand that you wanted to test me. You probably thought that I would leave Morten as soon as I could be well off myself. But when the student spoke, I thought how bad it is to betray a comrade, so I did not want to do it."

Bataki scratched his neck and looked embarrassed. Then they flew straight over the Cathedral and the city of learning, back to the geese.

Gorgo the Eagle

May 5 – 6

"There lies Stockholm, the city which floats on the water! Now I really know where I am," cried Down-Fine. Through haze and mist Nils glimpsed houses and spires in every direction. The geese were flying fast, and in order to view the city he had to turn around. Then it looked still more enchanted. The houses were white; the windows glowed like fire; everything swam on the water.

When the geese arrived at the island, Down-Fine's parents were boundlessly happy to see their daughter again. The wild geese were so well received that they decided to spend the day there.

The boy was sunning himself on a warm flat rock, when he heard Down-Fine cry, "Thumbkin! Thumbkin! Morten Gander is being torn to death by an eagle!" With lightning speed, Nils threw himself on Down-Fine's back. They found Morten bleeding and torn but still bravely fighting a golden eagle. The boy cried, "Quick, Down-Fine, summon Akka and the wild geese!"

Hardly had he said this when the eagle let Morten go. He gazed proudly at Thumbkin and said, "Give Akka greetings from Gorgo the Eagle. Tell her that I had never expected to find her or one of her flock out here among the seaward skerries."

When Nils conveyed to Akka the eagle's greeting she only said, "Oh yes," as though she were thinking of more important affairs. He thought this strange, but soon he too had other things to think about.

* * *

Bound with twine around his hands and feet, Nils Holgersson lay on the bottom of a wicker basket, covered with a well-secured lid. He could see nothing, because the fisherman who carried the creel held it under his arm. What had happened and what was in store for him?

The fisherman stopped and asked someone if the superintendent was home. "I think he is," answered an old man's voice. "What do you have with you today? A choice live seabird, as usual, Asbjörn?" —"Take a look yourself," Asbjörn said, and opened the lid. Terrified, the boy looked up into a bearded face. "How did you get hold of this one?" the old man asked, astounded. —"He came to me all by himself, straight out of the sky, when I was fishing this morning. I caught sight of the wild geese and fired a shot at them. I didn't hit any, of course. But instead, this one came plumping down into the water, so close that I only had to fish him out with my net. I was quick to tie him up. I thought right away that this would be something for the gentleman at Skansen."

The boy had heard about Skansen. Many old and interesting things had been collected there from the whole country. Was he himself now going to be exhibited in a cage so that people could come and stare at him as a freak? The boy suffered agony. He turned and twisted—and discovered a hole in the wicker near the bottom. Through it he could now look directly at a monkey clinging to a tree. That sight gave him strength. He got hold of his sheath knife and, at the risk of severing an artery, set about cutting the twine.

"Don't you realize that he is a supernatural creature?" Klement was asking.

But Nils did not hear any more. At that moment he was busy creeping out of the basket, stealing unseen in among the bushes, and hiding himself.

It was not difficult for him to make the time pass at Skansen. He got acquainted with the animals and made many friends. Since he had, after all, suffered a good deal in the cold, damp weather during the journey, he thought it might be a good thing that he had been forced to break off the trip. Besides, he had no other choice. But here Akka would never find him.

Then one day the boy happened to pass the eagle cage. It was built out in the open with iron bars and steel wire, and it was so big that a couple of trees found room inside. But the eagles sat motionless and silent, and their beautiful, dark plumage had become rumpled and dull. With a hopeless longing, they stared into the air.

One of the three eagles was a newcomer. Yet even he sat like the two others, although his plumage was still beautiful and shiny. All at once, "Gorgo! Gorgo!" the boy called up from the ground. The eagle hardly had strength to lower his gaze and asked faintly, "Who is calling me?" —"Gorgo! It is Thumbkin, who used to fly with the wild geese! Don't you recognize me?" —"Is Akka also captive?" asked the eagle. "No,

by this time all the others are probably safe in Lapland. I am the only one here. Can I help you in some way, Gorgo?" —"Don't disturb me, Thumbkin. I sit and dream that I am soaring around free in the heavens. I do not want to be awake." —"No, Golden Eagle, you must move around and follow what is happening. Otherwise you'll become just as wretched as the others," warned Nils. —"I wish I *were* like the other two," the eagle replied. "Nothing disturbs them."

In the half-lit night that followed, a strange rasping sound was heard from the roof of the eagle cage. It was Nils Holgersson, who clung there and filed away at a steel wire. Gorgo lifted his head. The other two were too listless; they did not move. "I am a big bird, Thumbkin," the eagle said after a while. "Give that up. You can never file apart so many wires." —"You sleep," said the boy, "and I'll keep on. You'll be totally destroyed if you stay here."

The next day the eagle moved around on the tree branches and flapped his wings to get the stiffness out of his body.

One early morning, just as the first streak of dawn was lighting the sky, Thumbkin awakened the eagle. "Try now, Gorgo." The eagle looked up. There was a big hole in the roof. The eagle threw himself against it, failed a couple of times, but then was safely out. He rose in proud flight against the sky and disappeared.

Little Thumbkin was left sitting there gazing after him with a melancholy expression. It was pleasant here, to be sure, and he felt at home in Skansen. He had no difficulty in making the time pass. But his thoughts were drawn every day to Morten Gander and his other traveling companions. The ground was green, the cherry trees were blossoming, birch and poplar had dressed themselves in shimmering silken leaves, peas and beans were sprouting up in their beds. "So it is probably warm in Lapland too," the boy thought. "If only I were sitting on the back of the gander and riding in warm, still air! If only I could meet Akka again . . ."

Suddenly the eagle swooped down from the sky and settled beside him on the roof of the cage. "I had to try my wings to see if they were still good for anything," said Gorgo. "Surely you didn't think that I planned to leave you behind in captivity?" And with that he grasped Nils Holgersson with his big talons and rose with him into the sky. Swiftly they sped toward the north.

Northward with Gorgo

June 7 – 16

Nils dangled from the eagle's claws for a long time and saw not a jot. Only when the eagle descended to rest on a stone beside a waterfall did he have a chance to look around again. Above them hurtled the white foaming wall of water, and all around them gushed the river.

"We are on our way to your traveling companions," Gorgo said. —"But Lapland is supposed to be dreadfully big. Perhaps you will not find them," Nils replied. —"I will find them. I'm going to tell you something. Then you'll understand."

So Gorgo told of a great eagle's nest on a rocky ledge high above a forgotten valley. Far below glittered a small round lake and on the grassy shore, among dwarf birches and willows, the wild geese were breeding. The eagles were reasonable, and never took so many geese that the birds did not dare to remain there. The geese in their turn found the marauders useful because they kept other enemies at a distance.

But then one evening the lead goose noticed that the eagles had not returned to their nest. The next day, in the morning stillness, mournful and angry shrieks were heard from the nest. The lead goose flew up high enough to look down into the nest. There lay a half-naked fledgling, crying. "Was that you? And Akka?" the boy interrupted. —"It was I, all right. I do not remember it myself, but Akka has often told about it. Now listen."

That eaglet was a real rascal. "Get food for me at once!" he yelled. "Don't sit and stare! It is disgraceful of my mother to let me starve. Food at once! Quickly!" The wild goose understood that the eagles had been shot. If the eaglet died, then the wild geese would have peace. But not to help an abandoned wretch—that went against

Akka's grain, you see. She flew away and was soon back with a freshly caught trout. Instead of thanks, the brat pecked at her. "It is a white grouse I want! Or a lemming. Don't forget that!" Akka only flew on her way and when she returned the fish had slipped down into the empty stomach of the young eagle. It became hard work to procure food for the greedy infant, who soon got the idea that Akka was his real mother.

One day she had to tell him, "Now comes the time when the geese shed their feathers. I cannot fly up here anymore with food. You will starve to death if you do not dare to hurl yourself down into the valley. There I can feed you as before." The eaglet did not reflect on this for one second, but hurled himself straight out into the air. He tumbled about a little, but got down. Thereafter he lived with the wild geese. Akka tried to raise him to be a good and gentle wild goose, until one day he became aware that he was really an eagle and had to live like one. Akka had been proud that an eagle was living in her flock. She became indignant when he wanted to live according to his own taste. "Behave as I have taught you," she ordered.

They were both proud, and neither wanted to give in.

"So Akka forbade me to show myself in her company any longer, and no one may speak to her about me," Gorgo concluded. Then he added, "However, I have never done any violence to a wild goose. You are supposed to stand high in Akka's favor and now I want you to make peace between us."

As the eagle and the boy flew farther north, there really wasn't very much to look at, only forests, rushing streams, glassy lakes. Along the shores there was one ironworks after another. Gorgo steered directly through the smoke so that Nils turned as black as a chimney sweep.

Farther north a huge dark cloud sailed up and sent a torrential downpour against the sea of forest. Here again, Gorgo flew

right on through, so that the chimney sweep got thoroughly washed.

Then the sun came out again and Gorgo settled down on a long, barren ridge. "Now I must go hunting," he said. "You won't be afraid if you have to wait for me here until evening?" —"Of course not," said Nils, but he did feel somewhat abandoned as he sat on a stone and looked around him . . .

It was plain that a forest fire had recently raged here, for there were black stumps still left among the flat rocks. After the fire, rainstorms had washed away much of the good soil. The boy found the place depressing and not even a frozen lingonberry could he find to eat.

Then he heard singing from the forest below. A procession of people soon came up along the ridge, with a banner at the head. A gay procession it was, teeming with children—an entire school of them off to plant trees. They carried hoes and spades and knapsacks of food. The teachers were along and the school porter too, with a wagonload of pine seedlings.

These small seedlings were meant to anchor the soil that remained after the fire so that new soil could form between the trees. One of the teachers said, "When some day your children see that forest, they will think that we were wise people to leave them such a fine inheritance."

One day Nils rode on Gorgo's back. He saw people and cattle emerging from every valley and every farm. All through the day were heard the songs of the herd maidens, the lowing of the animals, and the tinkling cowbells.

But the next day again there was only forest after forest. "It must take patience and still more patience for anyone to make a living from such land," Nils thought, and recalled the golden fields at home. Then Gorgo flew over a stretch of tree stumps. "This too is a sort of field. It was harvested last winter," he said. —"In Skåne," Nils replied, "we mow the grain in a few days, but this must take months even for the most hard-working people . . ."

They saw a splendid river in a broad valley, a prosperous district with timbered farmsteads. Endless masses of timber were floating down the river, but who looked after them? The boy could not believe that more than half would reach their goal. Then he caught sight of the lumbermen at work with their boat hooks. They were daring and resourceful men. They sauntered over the rocking timber heaps as though tramping the cottage floor or the farmyard at home. One lumberman stood quite calmly on a single log and steered it with an oar down the river. It raced ahead and Nils turned around on the eagle's back and watched for a long, long time.

Nils was awfully hungry. But it was not easy for Gorgo to get food for him. Every time they descended, the cries of the small birds alerted the people and the men would run for their guns. Nils felt really sorry for Gorgo, who was so hated.

Later, they flew over a valley and a river with a bridge which, in spite of the rain mist, looked more beautiful than any of the ones they had seen so far. There wasn't much traffic on the bridge, only a few cars and a woman walking with a little girl. When the woman caught sight of the eagle she stopped. As a joke she took out a freshly baked bun and held it high in the air. "If you want it, take it!" she said laughingly. Before she even realized what was happening, Gorgo had darted down like an arrow and grabbed it. "If I become a human being again, I will come up here and thank her," thought the boy. He had tears in his eyes . . .

Lapland

July – August

The eagle now flew with tremendous speed. "We are in Lapland," he said. Again Nils could see only forest and marsh, marsh and forest. It was as light as day, but it must have been night because the cranes stood asleep in the marshes. Yet the sun lay due north and shone straight in his face. "I must sleep awhile," he said, "otherwise I shall fall off." Gorgo flew down to a marsh and the boy climbed off but immediately felt himself grasped again by the eagle's talons. "You go to sleep, Thumbkin! The sunshine keeps me awake, and I'm going to continue the journey tonight," said the eagle. They swung up into the sky, while a moose stared after them, astonished.

When Nils awoke, he was lying alone at the bottom of a vast mountain valley. He got up and looked around. Then he noticed a curious structure high on a cliff ledge. "That must be the kind of eagle's nest that Gorgo . . ."

He did not even finish his thought, but tore the cap from his head, and cheered! This was the valley where the eagle lived on the rock ledge, and the wild geese on the bottom of the valley. He had arrived!

Slowly he wandered along, searching for his friends. It was absolutely still in the valley. The sun had not risen over the cliff walls, and Nils Holgersson understood that it was so early in the morning that the wild geese were not yet awake. He had not gone far when he stopped and smiled, because he saw something so beautiful. A wild goose lay asleep in a small nest on the ground and by her side stood her gander. He also slept, but it was obvious that he wanted to be close at hand in case of any danger.

Nils peeped into many thickets and found both strange geese and geese from his own flock, but he did not wake them. Finally he thought he saw something white gleam inside a thicket, and his heart began to thump with joy. Yes indeed, there was Down-Fine sitting daintily on some eggs and by her side stood the white gander. Even as he slept it was clear how proud he was to keep watch over his mate up here in the mountains of Lapland.

The boy did not want to wake him, either . . . And then, on a little hillock, he noticed something that resembled a gray tuft. It was Akka from Kebnekaise keeping watch over the valley.

"Good morning, Mother Akka! Please

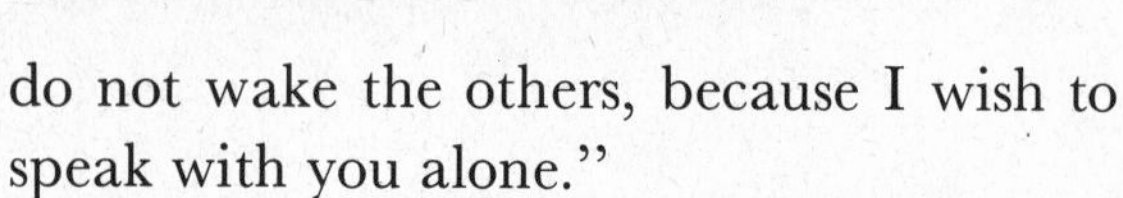

do not wake the others, because I wish to speak with you alone."

The old lead goose plunged head over heels down the slope toward the boy, grasped him and shook him, then stroked her bill along his body. She shook him again but said not one single word, in order not to wake the others.

Thumbkin kissed Mother Akka on both cheeks and told her how he had been taken to Skansen and how he had found the wretched eagle cage. "At first, I thought of filing apart the steel wire and letting him out. But later I remembered what a dangerous bird-eater and plunderer Gorgo is and then I didn't dare. Was that right, Mother Akka?" —"No, Nils. The eagles are more proud and freedom-loving than other animals, you see. When you have rested well, we two shall make a trip down to the great bird prison and set him free."

"I expected that from you, Mother Akka!" Nils said happily. "Now I can hear that you are still fond of the one you raised with so much trouble. And if you wish to say a word of thanks to the one who carried me here, you will find him up on the cliff ledge where you once found a poor, helpless eaglet . . ."

* * *

Nils Holgersson thought that he had never been in such a fair and glorious land. He had no worries other than preventing the swarms of mosquitoes from eating him up. He didn't see much of Morten Gander, since the big white one thought only of watching over Down-Fine. So Nils stayed in the company of Akka and Gorgo. The three whiled away many hours together, and went on many excursions. He stood on the snow-clad peak of Kebnekaise and looked down on the glaciers below the white summit. Akka showed him caves in the cliffs where the she-wolves reared their young.

But he had the most fun when, one day, he saw the Lapps make camp. After they had cut down some willow shrubs and evened out some tufts, the camp site was ready, and when they had hammered the tent poles securely in the ground and hung up the tent, the dwelling too was finished! With the interior there was just as little bother: fir sprays and a few reindeer skins on the floor, a chain attached to the top of the tent pole, from which to hang the kettle over the fire when the reindeer meat was cooked. The Lapps had wandered around up here for many hundreds of years without bothering about a better

shelter against storm and cold than thin tent walls.

Yes, it was an impressive land. Nils was glad that he had been able to visit it for an entire long summer. But as for wanting to live here permanently—no. He thought Akka was right when she said that the settlers should have left this land to the bears and the wolves, and to the Lapps, of course.

To the South, to the South!

September

Nils thought it was about time that the wild geese moved south.

Not only was it dark and cold and the food scarce but also he yearned for the day when he could go home with Morten Gander and become a human being again.

One morning the ground lay white as

far as he could see. The snow melted during the day, to be sure, but Akka gave the signal for departure. The wings of the goslings had grown out, so now they could travel.

Thirty-one wild geese flew southward in orderly formation. Feathers rustled, wings lashed the air with such clamor that one could hardly hear one's own voice. Akka from Kebnekaise flew at the head, followed by Yksi, Kaksi, Kolme, and Neljä in one row, and Viisi, Kuusi, Down-Fine,

and Morten, with Nils Holgersson, in the second. Behind them came twenty-two goslings.

The poor goslings, who had never made a long expedition, had difficulty keeping up. "Akka, Akka, Akka!" they cried in plaintive tones, "our wings are tired."

"The longer you keep it up, the better it will go," Akka said and flew on as before. And when the goslings had flown a couple of hours, they no longer complained of being tired. But then the youngsters cried piteously, "Akka! We are so hungry!" The lead goose replied, "Wild geese must learn

to eat air and drink wind!" And after they had flown awhile they no longer complained of hunger. The old geese called out the names of all the mountain peaks they passed so that the youngsters would learn them. The goslings replied in heart-rending tones, "Akka, Akka! We have no room in our heads for any more names!" —"The more that enters a head, the more room there is!" Akka answered.

The boy was very happy when he saw the first pine forest, the first gray mountain farm, the first goat, the first cat. And when he discovered a chapel, a small parsonage, and a little church village he thought them so pretty that he got tears in his eyes.

The bears rushed out when the wild geese came over and growled to their cubs, "Look at them. They are so afraid of a little cold that they don't dare stay home during the winter!" But the old wild geese had a reply ready. "Look at those creatures who lie asleep the whole winter rather than take the trouble to go south!"

The boy saw Lapps rounding up their reindeer in the mountains, moving down into the valleys. The wild geese called out, "Thanks for this summer!" And the reindeer answered, "A pleasant journey and come back safely!"

Then quickly, as they flew, the fog came rolling in. The geese descended on a green hillock where everything was dripping wet. As soon as Nils moved, there came a shower of drops from every blade of grass.

Then, through the mist, he glimpsed an observation tower. Up there he could probably find a dry resting place, so he asked Morten to fly him up and fetch him in the morning. But when he awoke, the geese were gone. No one answered from below.

The boy became quite upset. All kinds of misfortunes might befall Morten during the journey . . .

Suddenly Bataki stood beside him. Never had Nils thought that he would be so happy to see the raven again. "Akka sends you greetings," the raven said. "She spied some hunters on the mountain here, and did not dare to remain. But I shall take you to the flock."

High above the mists Bataki flew, in the brightest sunshine. When the mists cleared, they flew to a tree on the crest of a ridge and sat down, each one on his own branch.

"You probably don't know what kind of mound this is," Bataki said. "It is a burial mound, which was built over the first man to settle here." —"Perhaps you'll tell me about him while I eat," Nils said, munching on a grain of barley.

"I don't know much about him," Bataki answered. "He was a Norwegian and Härjulf was his name. He fell out with the Norwegian King and had to flee the country and enter the service of the Swedish King in Uppsala. This King refused to give him his sister for a wife, and so he ran away with her. Now he had so managed it that he could live neither in Norway nor in Sweden, and he did not want to move to foreign lands. 'There must be another way out,' he thought and departed with his wife and all his men for the vast empty forests to the north. There he founded a settlement."

Nils grew thoughtful. Bataki always had something special in mind when he told his stories. Then the raven continued, "Do you really know everything that the elf said to Akka?" —"Yes? It is odd, but you always make me feel so uncomfortable, Bataki." —"I think you'll be grateful to hear the elf's entire answer: you are to bring Morten home . . . so that your mother can put him on the slaughtering block!"

The boy started up and almost tumbled to the ground. "I hope that is your own wicked invention." —"Ask Akka," the raven answered. "By the way, there I see the flock coming. But do not forget this: there is a way out of every difficulty if only one can find it."

Akka could not deny that Bataki had told the truth. "You must not say anything to Morten," Nils said. "He is so brave and generous that he might do something rash if he heard." Akka promised.

After that the boy rode glum and silent and didn't care to see anything. "I shall travel with the wild geese all my life now, so I'll probably get to know this countryside only too well," he thought.

Journey Toward the Sea

October

The wild geese settled down for the night on a forest rise and the boy set off to find something to eat. Near to a small manor house Nils discovered a currant bush with long red clusters of fruit, and on the gravel path he suddenly saw a fine red apple. He sat down beside it, and cut out small pieces with his sheath knife. He thought, "To be an elf all your life might not be so bad if you could always find good food so easily. What if I were to stay here? How will I be able to explain to Morten that I cannot go home? It is probably best for us to separate . . ."

Then a tawny owl flew down onto the gravel path. "Well now! It's nice to meet a living creature," the boy said. "And what

is the name of this place, Mrs. Tawny Owl?" —"It is Mårbacka," the owl hissed, and suddenly she dug her claws into his shoulder and pecked at his eyes. He realized that his life was in danger and yelled for help with all his might. Immediately he heard steps behind him. The owl released her hold and flew up into the nearest tree. A lady was standing shaking her umbrella at the owl. "Thanks for your help!" Nils shouted. The lady looked most surprised, so he continued, "I am a human being like you. But an elf has bewitched me." —"That's the most extraordinary thing I have ever heard!" the lady said. "How did you get into such trouble?" The boy related everything that had happened to him, and he saw that she grew more and more astonished and delighted. "It was certainly fortunate that I should get to meet you here. I have long thought what fun it would be to write a story telling the schoolchildren all about Sweden. In such a book, of course, everything must be serious and absolutely true. It was so difficult that I was thinking of giving it up. But now I can write in the book exactly what you have told me. You have really helped me!"

After this, the boy began to get back his good spirits. He had spoken with a human being! The lady had given him a grain of hope and confidence. It was probably this which made him think of a way to prevent the big white gander from going home.

"Look how beautiful everything is," he said. "I'm sitting here thinking that we ought to go on abroad with the geese. It would be a pity not to see more of the world."

—"Surely you don't mean that!" the gander cried. For now that he had shown that he could make the Lapland journey, he was quite content with the thought of the goose pen in Holger Nilsson's cowshed. "I thought you wanted to show your mother and father what a fine boy you have become, Thumbkin!" he continued. As for himself, he had dreamt how lovely it would be to show Down-Fine and the goslings to all the other animals and to Mother Holger Nilsson herself.

The wild geese now passed over the lakes. "Look, look, Morten!" Nils cried again. "Have you ever seen anything like it?" High over the roadway a big boat glided in a canal, glided as if in the air, and above it was a railway where a train was racing along, and then—truly!—above *that* was a bridge on which people stood looking down on all this. "This is the Dalsland Canal," cried the older geese. "Such things you don't find in Skåne," Nils said. —"Well," Morten answered, "if you absolutely must go on, I shall not part from you." —"That's the answer I thought you would give me," said Nils, and one could hear relief in his voice. The sun was down at the horizon and sometimes disappeared behind one hill or another, but the wild geese charged on.

The boy felt a great sense of peace and security when he viewed the free, infinite

sea and the mild evening sun. "It is not worth while to be sad, Nils Holgersson," said the sun. "The world is glorious to live in, for both great and small. And it is good to be free and untroubled and to have the open sky before you."

The next day, the wild geese flew down along the coast. Blue and green boats with furled sails lay bobbing in the harbors. A swarm of gulls suddenly raced off southward, the cormorants following in leaden flight. The boy saw dolphins glide through the sea, and a herd of seals slither down from a skerry and also steer south. Fishing boats were made ready and the dry nets were carried on board. Soon the Sound was filled with brown sails and the chuffing of motors. "What is up? What is up?" the young geese asked, and a long-tailed duck replied in passing, "Herring! Herring!"

The wild geese reached the wide fjord just as the fish rushed in from the west. Where the water rippled and darkened, the people in the boats knew the herring had stopped, and there they set out their long nets in a circle. The wild geese circled around several times so that Nils might really see everything.

But soon he asked that they travel on. He did not say why, but Akka, perhaps, guessed what he felt. There were many fine, impressive-looking men among the fishermen. They looked just as daring and bold as every boy hopes to be when he grows up. Perhaps sitting and watching them was not so pleasant for someone who would never himself grow taller than a herring . . .

Now the boy noticed more and more boats down on the sea, and all of them seemed to be coming from or going to a particular place. Akka cried, "Göteborg!" and even though the geese were flying high, Nils could see that this was a rich trade center. There lay the shipyards where the ocean liners were built, and there were moored hundreds of ships along endless docks.

The wild geese stopped to feed for a while and had a gay time with other flocks. Nils, on the other hand, was not happy. "If I had only put Skåne behind me so that there was no longer anything to hope for . . ."

At last they set off into Skåne. The boy began to lean down over the neck of the gander and did not lift his eyes from the ground. When the plain extended all the way to the horizon, he felt both glad and anxious. "Now I cannot be far from home!"

Home at Last

November 8

During a midday rest Akka came up to Nils. "The weather is calm now, so I think we shall travel across the Baltic Sea tomorrow," she said. —"Oh," he replied shortly, for his throat was so tight that he could barely speak. He had, perhaps, still hoped that he might be released from the enchantment. "I thought you might like to go home for a little while," said Akka.

—"It is probably best not to . . ." said Nils, but it was clear from his voice that he was happy over the thought. "If the gander stays with us, no harm is likely to come to him," Akka continued. "I think you should find out how things are at home. Perhaps you can help them in some way." —"Yes, I should have thought of that already," Nils answered eagerly, and the next moment they were on their way. In a short time, he recognized Holger Nilsson's farm, and Akka came down behind the stone wall which surrounded it. Nils Holgersson quickly climbed up on the stones. "How much the same everything looks. It seems like yesterday that I saw you come flying."

"Does your father have a gun?" Akka asked, worried. —"Of course. It was because of the gun that I stayed home from church that Sunday." —"Then I dare not wait for you. You should come and meet us early tomorrow morning." —"Oh no, Mother Akka, don't go yet!" The boy had an odd feeling that something might happen, that they might never meet again. "You have probably seen that I am sorry I can't become big again," he said, "but don't think that I regret having gone along with you. No, I would rather never become human again than have missed making this journey."

Akka drew a couple of breaths before

she answered. "You talk as though we were never to meet again, but we shall see each other tomorrow, you know." She spread her wings, then turned back and stroked Thumbkin up and down a couple of times with her bill. And then she flew on her way.

It was silent on the farm. Nils hurried to the cowshed. He knew that there he could get the best information.

Without fear, he ran into the stall. "Good day, May-Rose! How are Father and Mother and all of you here on the farm?"

May-Rose started up and seemed about to gore him, but then she took time to look at him more closely. Yes, he was just as small and dressed in the same way he had been when he left. But still, he looked different. He was lithe and alert, not a lazy dullard. His eyes shone, and he seemed full of high spirits. May-Rose was glad when she saw him. "Moo!" she bellowed. "Welcome home. They said you had changed, but I could hardly believe it. Your parents have had only troubles since you went off. The worst is the new horse, who has something wrong with him which no one understands. He cannot work, and it's impossible to sell him. They had to dispose of Star and Golden Lily instead."

"I imagine Mother was sorry that Morten had flown away," the boy said. —"Yes, she was. Mostly because she thought you had stolen him. But you should know that she still mourns you as one mourns the loss of one's most precious possession."

In the stable was a handsome new horse who wasn't difficult to talk to. "I must have the point of a knife in my foot, because it hurts so I cannot walk. The doctor cannot find it." —"Perhaps I can help," said Nils. "May I scratch a little on your hoof with my knife?"

He was barely finished when he heard the voices of Father and Mother out in the yard. How troubled they sounded! "If I cannot make the horse well soon, we may have to give up the farm," Father said. —"But where will the boy go if he returns,

poor and wretched?" Mother said. "If I only had him here, I would not ask for anything more." —"Yes, then it would be easy to carry on," Father replied.

Father walked into the stable, and Nils had to creep quickly into a corner. As usual, Holger Nilsson lifted the foot of the horse to try to find out what was wrong. "But what is this? Here are some letters carved—'Take the iron out of the foot.'

Indeed, I think there *is* something here!"

In the meantime Morten had not been able to resist the temptation to show Down-Fine and the goslings how well off he had been as a tame goose. They alighted in the farmyard, and he proudly showed off all its glories. Since the door to the cowshed stood open, he led the way into the pen. "It is not dangerous," he said. "Look what fine grain there is in the trough!" Then the door slammed shut, and Down-Fine cried out as Mother fastened the hasp . . .

"Father! Come here and see!" cried Mother. "The gander is here with seven wild geese!" —"And I have discovered what is the matter with the horse." Father said. "I believe our luck has changed. But best of all, it wasn't Nils who stole the gander. It is almost a pity that we have to butcher them this very night in order to get them to town in time. You know there will be a holiday in a few days. Come and help me carry them into the cottage."

A few moments later, the boy saw Father and Mother enter the house carrying Down-Fine and Morten. The gander cried, "Thumbkin! Come and help me!" as he used to do when he was in danger.

Nils Holgersson heard him, of course, but nevertheless remained in the stable doorway. Not because it would have helped him if Morten were laid on the butcher's block—this he did not even remember at that moment—but because he would have to show himself to Father and Mother. "They have a hard enough time already without this," he thought. "Do I have to cause them more sorrow?"

But when the cottage door closed, Nils came to life. He raced across the farmyard, jumped up on the oak plank in front of the entrance, and ran into the entryway. Here he slipped out of his wooden shoes from force of habit and approached the door. But he couldn't raise his hand to knock. He so dreaded showing himself to Mother and Father in his present form . . . "Remember, this concerns Morten, who has been your best friend ever since you stood here the last time," he then said to himself. He remembered all that he and the gander had been through on frozen lakes and stormy seas and among dangerous beasts. Then he felt gratitude and love in his heart. He conquered his dread and pounded on the door. It slid open.

The Farewell

November 9

Early next morning the boy wandered down to the shore, east of the fishing village. He was alone. He had tried to wake Morten Gander, but the big white one had not said a word, and only went back to sleep again.

He himself was still in a kind of daze. Sometimes he felt like an elf, sometimes like a human being . . .

It looked as though it would be a lovely, clear day. He was glad that the geese would have a fine crossing. "I hope those aren't

"Mother, you must not touch the gander!" he cried, and immediately Morten and Down-Fine let out a cry of joy, so he knew that they were still alive.

Mother also uttered a cry of joy. "My, how big and handsome you have become!" she exclaimed, and let the goose go.

The boy had not entered the cottage but was still standing on the threshold, like one who isn't sure how he will be received. "God be praised that I have you back again!" Mother said. "Come in! Come in!" —"You are welcome," Father said. And not one more word could he get out.

But Nils still lingered on the threshold. He could not understand that they were so happy to see him in his present condition. But then Mother threw her arms around him and pulled him into the room, and he realized what had taken place.

"Mother and Father, I am big! I am a human being again!"

my geese departing without saying farewell." He stationed himself on the outermost edge of the shore, so that they could see him plainly.

One flock slowed and soared back and forth, searching. It was the right one. But why did they not swoop down by his side? He heard Akka cry, but he could not understand what she said. Now what? Had the geese changed their language? He tried to bring out a call that would lure them down to him. But imagine, his tongue failed him! He could not produce the right sound. He waved his cap, shouted and leapt. But this only frightened them, and they flew out to sea. Then he finally understood. They did not recognize him. He could not call them to his side, because a human being cannot speak the language of birds.

But presently he heard a rush of wings. Akka had found it hard to leave Thumbkin. She had turned back, and now that the boy was sitting still she dared to come closer. Perhaps something had suddenly shown her who he was. She settled down on the sand beside him.

The boy cried out with joy and clasped old Akka in his arms. The other wild geese also came and stroked their bills against him and crowded around. They cackled and chattered and warmly wished him good fortune. He spoke to them also and thanked them for the wonderful journey he had been allowed to make in their company.

All at once the wild geese became strangely quiet and drew away from him. It was as though they were saying, "Alas, he is human! He does not understand us. We do not understand him . . ."

And though the boy was happy that he had been freed from the enchantment, he felt this change bitterly. He sat down on the sand and covered his face with his hands. What was the use of gazing after them . . .

Finally the boy got up and went over to Akka. He fondled and patted her.

CO. SCHOOLS
C690339

Then he walked inland across the shore. For he knew, of course, that the sorrow of birds never lasts long, and he wanted to part from them while they were still sad over losing him.

On the embankment he turned around and watched the flocks of birds winging out over the sea, sounding their inviting calls. Only one flock of geese traveled silently as far as he could follow it with his eyes.

The formation was even and orderly. The speed was good and the wingstrokes strong and powerful. The boy felt such a longing for the ones flying away that he almost wished that he were still Thumbkin, who could ride over land and sea with a flock of wild geese.

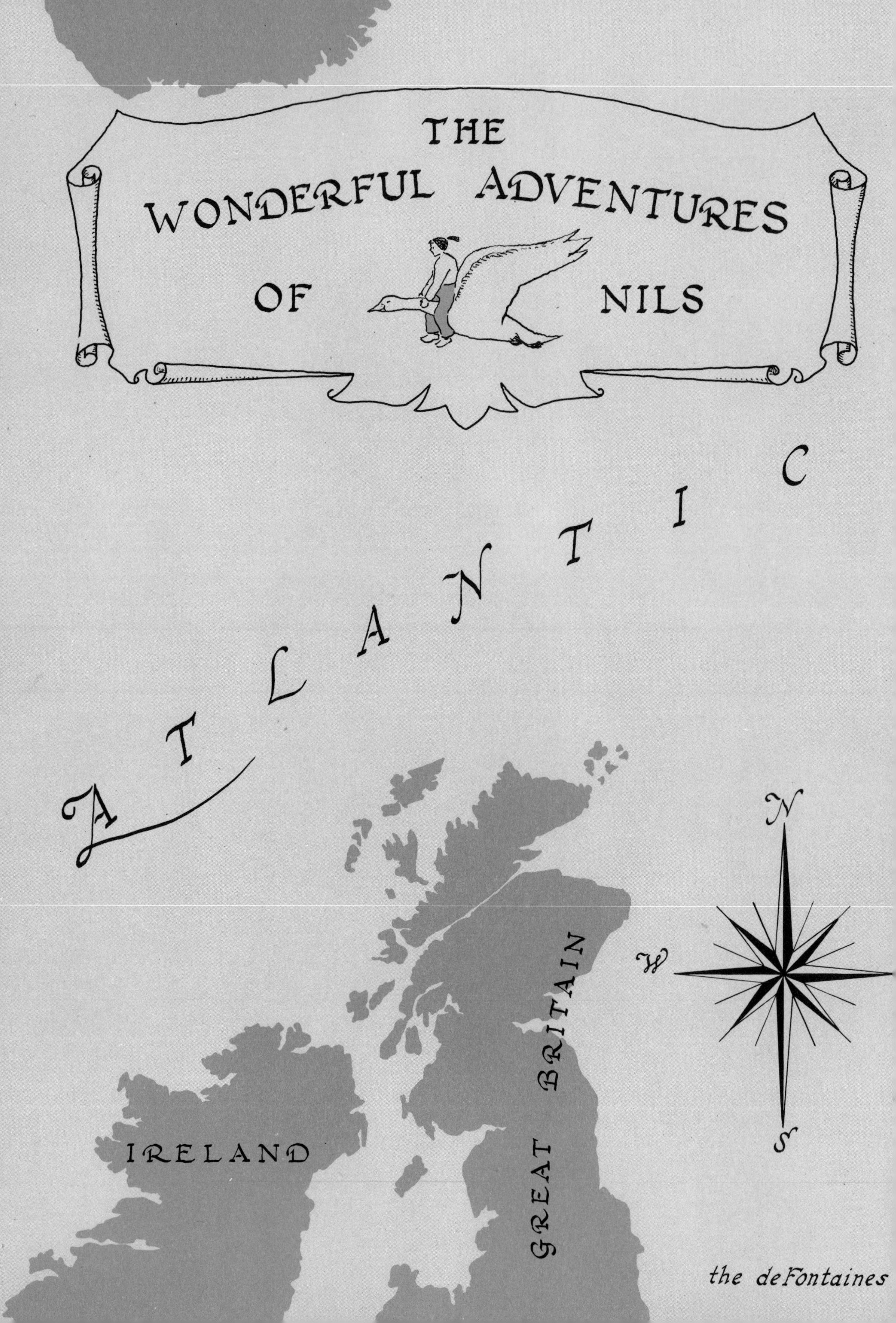
ICELAND
THE
WONDERFUL ADVENTURES
OF NILS
ATLANTIC
GREAT BRITAIN
IRELAND
N
W
S
the deFontaines